QUEEN OF PENTACLES

SHORT, SINGLE MOTHER, CURVY GODDESS, PROTECTOR HERO, MAGICAL REALM ROMANCE

TAROT FANTASIES SERIES
BOOK SIX

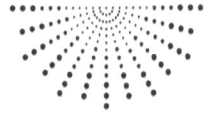

JAX WILDER

RAINBOW QUARTZ PUBLISHING

Published by Rainbow Quartz Publishing

Edmonds WA, 98026

ISBN: 978-1-961714-52-6 First Edition: 2024

Cover design by Miranda Townsend

Interior design by Miranda Townsend

Tarot Card description by Lorelai Hamilton from the book Teenage Tarot – used with permission.

For permissions or inquiries, please contact:

Rainbow Quartz Publishing rainbowquartzpublishing@gmail.com

RQPublishing.com

If it makes you smile, I've done my job.

Everyone Deserves Healthy Relationships Free of Domestic Violence

If you or someone you know are need help, call the National domestic Violence Hotline at 800-799-7233.

QUEEN OF PENTACLES

"Embrace the abundance that surrounds you," Queen of Pentacles.

Key Words and Phrases

Nurturing abundance and prosperity
Practicality and resourcefulness
Grounded and down-to-earth approach
Financial security and stability
Domestic harmony and comfort
Generosity and nurturing care
Connection to nature and the earth
Self-sufficiency and independence
Fertility and growth in all aspects of life

The Queen of Pentacles is about being grounded and caring. She's the ultimate provider, always making sure everyone is well cared for. She's the one who bakes the most delicious cookies, tends to the garden, and somehow always knows exactly what everyone needs.

When this queen sets her mind on something, she not only makes it happen but ensures it's done with love and attention to detail. She's the friend who always has a spare umbrella, the co-worker who brings in homemade snacks, and the family member who makes sure holidays are extra special. When you see the Queen of Pentacles in a reading, it's a reminder to embrace your nurturing side.

—Lorelai Hamilton, author of *Teenage Tarot* and *Tarot Tales & Magic Spells*

QUEEN of PENTACLES

CHAPTER ONE

I pushed open the door to the Arcane Room, the little bell tinkling overhead, its familiar sound feeling like a distant echo in a hollow, empty place inside me. Normally, the scent of incense and old books grounded me, bringing a sense of comfort, but today, I felt nothing. I wasn't here to lose myself in the atmosphere. I was here because I needed something more than an escape. I needed a reminder that I could still be strong.

Rose was with her father this weekend, and the silence in my apartment had been suffocating. Instead of relishing the quiet, all I could do was worry—worry about what kind of games he was playing with her, what lies he was planting in her innocent mind. Every time she was with him, I felt like I was losing a part of her, and the helplessness gnawed at me, keeping me awake at night. I was doing everything I could to build a stable life for Rose, but it always felt like trying to fill a bucket with a hole in the bottom—no matter how much I poured in, it was never enough.

"Melanie, darling," Ms. Vesper's voice broke through my thoughts, warm and soothing as always. She was arranging a few small bottles on the shelves, each one labeled in her neat, precise handwriting. "What a lovely surprise. How are you?"

I smiled weakly as I approached, though I doubted it reached my eyes. Ms. Vesper had been a lifeline for me once, back when I was barely holding it together. Just seeing her felt like a balm on the wound that had been bleeding inside me for years. "I've been better," I admitted, my voice betraying just how tired I was. "I wanted to come by and thank you in person. I don't know if I've ever really told you how much it meant… everything you did for me."

Ms. Vesper paused, her soft gaze fixed on me as if she could see straight through to the heart of my exhaustion. "You're very welcome, dear. But you got yourself out of that dark place. I just gave you a nudge."

I shook my head. "No, you did more than that. You helped me when I was at my lowest, when I didn't even know which way was up. When my ex was manipulating me, controlling every aspect of my life-refusing to let me have the car, controlling the money, isolating me. You were the one who saw through the lies, who got me in contact with Dove House. They gave me a way out when I thought I was stuck with him forever. I don't think I could've done it without you."

Ms. Vesper's eyes softened further, and she placed a gentle hand over mine. "You were never as trapped as you felt. But I'm glad I could be there to help you see it."

My throat tightened, and I looked down, struggling to hold back the tears that threatened to spill over. "I'm out of the house now, and I'm thankful for that every day. But…" My voice cracked, and I forced myself to take a breath before continuing. "I've never felt so tired in my life. I'm working every extra minute I can to pay for a lawyer, because without one, I feel like I'm failing Rose. He's making everything as difficult as possible. Refusing to pay child support unless there are strings attached— money if I give him our daughter. And his lawyer… she lies for him, manipulates the court. It's like fighting a battle with no end."

Ms. Vesper's expression darkened slightly, her hand still resting on mine as if to keep me anchored. "I can't imagine how difficult this must be for you, my dear."

"My cup's empty," I confessed quietly, my voice

barely above a whisper. "I'm running on fumes. The only bright spot in all of this is Rose, but I'm too exhausted to be the mother she needs. I take showers just so I can cry without her hearing. It's… it's like I've fought so hard, and I'm still losing."

There was a long silence between us, the weight of my words settling in the air. Ms. Vesper watched me closely before she spoke again, her voice softer than before. "Melanie, I know what it's like to feel that kind of exhaustion, to be so worn down by the fight that you can't see a way out. A long time ago, I was in a situation similar to yours."

I blinked, surprised by the confession. Ms. Vesper had always seemed so strong, so untouchable. "You were in an abusive relationship?"

She nodded slowly, her eyes clouded with memories. "Yes. Many years ago. He controlled me the way your ex controls you. The money, my time, my life. everything. I had no freedom. I was so beaten down, I didn't think I'd ever be free of him. But eventually… he got what was coming to him."

I swallowed, my curiosity getting the better of me. "What happened?"

Ms. Vesper smiled faintly, a glint of something dark in her eyes. "I cursed him."

I blinked, taken aback. "Cursed him?"

"Yes," she said simply. "And he never had the chance to hurt anyone again."

I shifted in my seat, unsure of how to respond. "I thought cursing someone was… you know, bad?"

Ms. Vesper's smile deepened. "Cursing someone has a cost, Melanie. But I was willing to pay that cost to protect myself, to reclaim my life. You've already started to take back your life, and you'll find your way out of this darkness. Sometimes, the universe demands justice, and it's up to us to deliver it. Just remember-whatever happens, you don't have to face it alone."

I shivered slightly at her words, a small spark of hope flaring in my chest. Maybe justice would come. Maybe I just had to hold on a little longer. "I hope you're right," I whispered, feeling the faintest stirrings of strength return to me.

Ms. Vesper gave me one last comforting smile. "I am, Melanie. Now, let's fill that empty cup of yours. You can't pour from it if you're dry."

I nodded, grateful for her words, for her presence. Maybe I wasn't as lost as I thought.

Ms. Vesper was quiet for a moment before she spoke again. "I have something special for you, if you have about twenty minutes to spare."

I looked at her, surprised by the offer. "I suppose I do," I said, glancing at my watch. I wasn't due to pick up Rose for a few hours yet. "What do you have in mind?"

She smiled, a mysterious glint in her eye, and

pulled out a deck of tarot cards from a drawer beneath the counter. "How about a little guidance?" She began to shuffle the deck, the cards whispering against each other like secrets being shared.

I watched as she laid the cards out in a neat fan on the counter. "Pick one," she said, her voice soothing.

I hesitated for a moment before passing my hand over the cards, feeling a strange pull toward one in particular. I plucked it from the lineup and handed it to Ms. Vesper. She turned it over, revealing the Queen of Pentacles.

A soft smile touched her lips. "The Queen of Pentacles," she said gently. "She represents a woman who is nurturing, practical, and devoted to those she loves. She's a caretaker, someone who gives endlessly to others but often forgets to care for herself."

I swallowed hard, the truth of her words hitting too close to home. "That sounds familiar."

Ms. Vesper placed the card down carefully, then led me toward the back of the store. "Come with me. I think you need some time to yourself, Melanie. Time to remember that you deserve to be cared for too. It's hard to take care of other's when your own cup is empty."

She opened a door to a small, white room. The

only thing in it was a black leather chaise lounge, its surface gleaming under the soft light.

"Drink this," she said, handing me a cup of steaming tea. "It will help you relax. Think of this as some much-needed me time. Only twenty minutes will pass while you're in the simulation, but it should feel much longer. You'll have full control over your experience."

I looked at her, confused. "Simulation?"

Ms. Vesper smiled reassuringly. "Trust me, Melanie. Just relax. This is for you."

I hesitated, but something in her voice, in the way she looked at me, made me trust her. I took the tea, signing a waiver she handed me with a shaky hand, and then slowly leaned back on the chaise lounge. I closed my eyes, the tea's warmth spreading through me, and let out a long, slow breath.

When I opened my eyes again, I wasn't in the white room anymore. I was sitting in a chair by a lake, the water calm and clear, reflecting the lush greenery that surrounded it. The air was fresh, filled with the sounds of nature—birds singing, leaves rustling in the gentle breeze. It was peaceful, a world away from the chaos of my life.

I got up slowly, walking to the end of a nearby dock and sitting on the edge, dipping my feet into the cool water. It felt like the world had been washed away, leaving only this moment of quiet.

"Mind if I join you?" a deep, smooth voice asked from behind me.

I turned to see a man standing there, tall with dark hair streaked with silver. He was probably twenty years older than me, and every bit of him dripped with sex appeal. His presence was magnetic, drawing me in without even trying.

CHAPTER TWO

I took a deep breath, letting the cool air fill my lungs as I turned to face the man who had just spoken. He was even more striking up close —tall, broad shoulders tapering down to a chiseled waist, his dark hair streaked with silver at the temples. His eyes, a deep, molten brown, seemed to hold a thousand secrets. Everything about him radiated confidence, the kind that only comes from knowing exactly who you are and what you're capable of.

"Mind if I join you?" His voice was smooth, tinged with a faint Hispanic accent that sent a shiver down my spine.

"Please," I said, trying to keep my voice steady despite the sudden flutter in my chest. "I'm Melanie."

"Diago," he introduced himself as he rolled up his

pants and sat down beside me, dipping his feet into the water. "So, what brings you to this little utopia, Melanie?"

I stared out at the serene lake, the water shimmering under the soft light. "Someone told me that in order to take care of other people, I have to take care of myself first."

Diago nodded, a small smile playing on his lips. "That's true. Self-care is important, especially for a queen like you."

I huffed a laugh, though it held no humor. "I don't feel much like a queen these days."

His gaze drifted over my body, his eyes lingering on the curves I usually tried to hide. "You should," he said, his voice low and intense. "You're beautiful, Melanie. Every curve, every line of your body is a testament to the life you've brought into this world. That's its own kind of magic."

Heat bloomed under my skin at his words, a mixture of embarrassment and arousal. It had been so long since someone had spoken to me like that, since someone had looked at me and seen something more than just a tired, overwhelmed single mom.

I swallowed hard, my throat suddenly dry. "How does this place work exactly?" I asked, needing to shift the focus away from the way his words were making my body respond.

Diago leaned back on his hands, his muscles

flexing beneath his shirt. "Everything in the Arcane Room stays in the Arcane Room. This place was conjured from your mind, Melanie. Everything you see, everything you feel, it's all here for your pleasure. Your desire."

I tilted my head, taking in everything he was saying, how real this place felt despite knowing logically it was a dream. "Is that so?" I murmured, my voice coming out breathier than I intended.

"Yes," he replied, his voice like silk as he stood up, his fingers deftly unbuttoning his shirt. He slipped it off, revealing a chest that looked like it had been carved from stone, every muscle defined, every inch of him screaming raw, masculine power.

I couldn't tear my eyes away as he undid his pants, sliding them down his legs and stepping out of them, leaving him in nothing but a pair of boxer briefs that clung to his powerful thighs and did little to hide the impressive bulge beneath. He was every inch the fantasy I hadn't allowed myself to have in years.

"Are you going to join me for a swim?" he asked, his eyes dark with promise.

I bit my lip, my mind a whirl of thoughts. It felt too real, too vivid, but I knew somewhere deep down that this was all just a dream, a way to escape the relentless stress of my everyday life. When would I ever have a chance like this again?

"When in Rome..." I said softly, standing up and slowly peeling off my top. I kicked off my shoes and slid my pants down, stepping out of them as the cool air kissed my skin. The water was inviting, and before I could second-guess myself, I dove in after Diago.

The water was perfect, cool but not cold, and it felt incredible against my heated skin. When I surfaced, Diago was there, holding out a hand to me. I took it, and he pulled me close, our bodies brushing against each other under the water.

"Do you want to see something magical?" he asked, his voice a seductive whisper against my ear.

"Of course," I replied, feeling myself start to relax into the experience. For once, I wasn't thinking about anything else—not my ex, not the bills, not even Rose. It was just me and this impossibly sexy man in a place that felt like it was made just for me.

"Follow me," Diago said, releasing my hand and swimming out toward a small cove nestled along the edge of the lake. I followed him, marveling at how the water seemed to embrace me, its temperature perfect, its clarity so pure I could see straight to the bottom.

We reached the cove, and I gasped. There, cascading down from a rocky ledge, was a waterfall. The water flowed into the lake, sparkling in the light, creating a mist that hung in the air like a fine veil.

"How is this possible?" I asked, incredulous. "This lake shouldn't have a waterfall."

Diago smiled, turning to face me. "This is the Arcane Room, Melanie. You desired a waterfall, so there is one."

I couldn't help but smile back, the wonder of it all breaking through the last of my defenses. "I could get used to this."

We swam behind the waterfall, the water cascading over us, the noise of it roaring in my ears. I laughed, a genuine sound that I hadn't heard from myself in far too long. It felt good, like shedding a heavy coat I'd been carrying for years.

Diago was close now, his body radiating heat despite the cool water. He looked at me, his eyes filled with something dark and hungry. "I want to take care of you, Melanie. Remind you of the sexy, sensual woman you are."

His words sent a jolt of desire straight through me, and I found myself leaning into him, craving the contact. For so long, I'd forgotten what it felt like to be touched, to be wanted. I wasn't just a mother, or a survivor—I was still a woman with desires, with needs.

My thoughts drifted to Rose for a moment, guilt trying to claw its way back in. But as if reading my mind, Diago whispered, "Rose will still be there when you're done here. And you'll be a better mother for taking this time for yourself."

I nodded, knowing he was right, even if it felt selfish. "I want a lot of things that I can't have here," I said, the admission raw on my tongue. "It feels selfish being here at all."

Diago cupped my face, his thumb brushing over my cheek. "You give of yourself all day, every day, to anyone who needs it. Now is the time for you and only you. Be selfish, Melanie. Tell me what you want."

I looked into his eyes, and the answer was right there, burning in the back of my throat. "I want you."

He smiled, slow and wicked, and it sent a thrill down my spine. "I'm yours."

He moved closer, his lips finding mine in a kiss that was deep and consuming, a fire that spread through my entire body. It was the first time I'd kissed someone since leaving my ex, and it felt like coming alive after years of merely existing. Diago's tongue found mine, and I lost myself in the kiss, in the taste of him, in the way his hands moved down my body as if he already knew every curve, every dip.

His hands cupped my breasts, his fingers tracing circles around my nipples before taking one into his hand, squeezing just right. I moaned against his mouth, the pleasure like a drug I hadn't realized I'd been craving. We moved against a rock wall, the waterfall just inches from us, its roar a backdrop to the sound of my own heartbeat thundering in my ears.

Diago's hands slid lower, parting my legs underwater, finding the heat between them with a precision that made me gasp. I was lost in the sensations, in the way his fingers moved against me, stroking, teasing, driving me closer and closer to the edge.

My hands roamed his body, tracing the hard lines of his muscles, feeling the strength in him, the power. When I found his arousal, I couldn't help but compare—he was so much bigger, so much more than the small, unremarkable cock my ex had. With my ex, I had to pretend, to fake pleasure just so he would leave me alone for a while. But with Diago, there was no need to pretend. Every touch, every stroke was real, driving me mad with want.

As if sensing my thoughts, Diago growled low in his throat. "Any man who hurts you will have to deal with me. I'll protect you, Melanie. And I'll teach you how to protect yourself."

His words heated me from the inside out, and before I knew what I was doing, I moved to straddle him right there in the water. Diago's hands gripped my hips as he maneuvered me over his throbbing cock, slowly stretching me until I took all of him. The sensation was overwhelming, the full-ness, the way he filled me so completely, so perfectly.

He moved slowly at first, letting me adjust, his lips finding my breast, taking it into his mouth as he began to move. The pleasure was exquisite, every stroke sending ripples of ecstasy through me. He picked up speed, his hips driving into me with a power that left me breathless.

"You're so beautiful," he murmured against my skin, his voice thick with desire. "So sexy, Melanie. Every inch of you is perfection."

I moved with him, matching his rhythm, feeling every thrust, every plunge into my core. It was like nothing I had ever felt before—each movement seemed to reach deeper, unraveling the tension I had held in my body for so long. The coiling heat inside me built rapidly, my body responding to him in ways I had forgotten it could.

My nails dug into his back as the pressure became almost too much to bear. The waterfall roared beside us, but all I could hear was the pounding of my heart, the soft gasps and moans escaping my lips, and the primal growls from Diago as he took me higher and higher.

"Diago," I gasped, my voice catching as the plea-sure mounted, "I—I can't—"

"Let go," he whispered, his breath hot against my

ear as he thrust harder, his grip on me tightening. "Come for me, Melanie. Show me how good it feels."

His words, his touch, his everything pushed me over the edge, and I exploded around him, my body shuddering with the force of the best orgasm I'd ever experienced. It was like the world itself shattered, leaving only the two of us in this moment of pure, unadulterated pleasure.

Diago followed me into the abyss, his body tensing as he found his own release, groaning my name as he emptied himself inside me. We clung to each other, riding out the waves of pleasure until they finally began to subside, leaving us both breathless and trembling in the afterglow.

For a long moment, we just stayed there, our bodies still intertwined, the cool water lapping gently around us as we caught our breath. I felt a sense of peace wash over me, a deep, bone-deep contentment that I hadn't felt in years. It was as if the weight I had been carrying had been lifted, even if only for a little while.

Diago pulled back slightly, just enough to look into my eyes. His gaze was warm, tender, filled with something that made my heart ache in the best way. He brushed a stray lock of hair away from my face, his thumb grazing my cheek.

"You are incredible, Melanie," he said softly. "Never forget that."

I smiled, feeling tears prick at the corners of my eyes—not from sadness, but from the overwhelming relief and gratitude I felt in that moment. "Thank you," I whispered, my voice thick with emotion. "I didn't realize how much I needed this."

He kissed me gently, a lingering kiss that felt like a promise of more to come. When he pulled back, his eyes sparkled with that mischievous glint again.

"And now," he said, his voice light and teasing, "let's explore this magical place a little more. Who knows what other surprises the Arcane Room has in store for you?"

I laughed, genuine and full, a sound that echoed off the rocks around us. "I think I could get used to this," I said, echoing my earlier words.

Diago grinned, taking my hand and leading me back through the water, back toward the lake's edge. As we swam, I felt lighter, freer, the worries of my life outside the Arcane Room fading into the background. For the first time in a long time, I allowed myself to just be—no worries, no responsibilities, just the simple pleasure of existing in this moment, with this man who had brought me back to life.

And as we emerged from the water, the sun warming our skin, I knew that this was only the beginning. The Arcane Room had given me more than just an escape—it had given me a taste of the woman I used to be, the woman I could still be. And I wasn't about to let her go.

CHAPTER THREE

*B*ack on the dock, the water still rippling from our swim, I felt like a different person. It was as if I had shed a layer of my old self and was now standing on the edge of something new, something I had almost forgotten I could be. Diago's presence only intensified the sensation, his every movement, every look, dripping with a raw, sensual energy that made me feel alive.

He turned to me, his dark eyes holding a spark of mischief. "I want to show you something," he said, his voice smooth like honey.

I was already feeling lighter, more carefree than I had in years. Whatever the Arcane Room had in store, I was ready for it. "Okay," I said, smiling up at him. "Show me."

With a snap of his fingers, everything changed.

The cool air of the lake transformed into the warmth of a summer festival, and I found myself dressed in what could only be described as Renaissance fair attire. My dress was a deep burgundy, low-cut and fitted perfectly to accentuate my breasts. The skirt flowed around me in rich waves of fabric, brushing against my legs with each step. Diago was similarly dressed, his shirt open to reveal his muscular chest, his pants hugging his form in all the right places.

"My lady," he said with a charming smile, taking my hand. "Just beyond this grove of trees, there's a fair taking place. I thought you might enjoy it."

We walked hand in hand through the trees, and as we emerged on the other side, I gasped in delight. The fair was bustling with life—people dressed in vibrant costumes, dancing to lively music, and feasting on foods that smelled absolutely divine. The scent of roasting meat, fresh bread, and sweet pastries filled the air, making my mouth water.

Diago watched me, his gaze filled with a mix of amusement and satisfaction. "You can have anything you want here, Melanie," he said softly. "But first, I would be honored if you would dance with me."

My heart swelled at the invitation. I had always loved dancing, especially at Ren fairs, where I could lose myself in the music and the joy of the moment. It had been so long since I'd allowed myself that kind of happiness, that kind of freedom. "I'd love to," I said, my smile growing wider.

He led me to the center of the clearing where others were already dancing, their laughter and movements infectious. As the music swelled, Diago pulled me close, his hand resting on the small of my back, the other clasping mine. We moved together, his steps guiding me effortlessly through the dance. It felt natural, like we had done this a thousand times before.

I laughed, the sound light and free, feeling a piece of myself returning. This was who I had been before my ex had twisted me into someone else—someone smaller, quieter, less joyful. He had mocked my love for Ren fairs, for costumes, for anything that brought color into life. He'd called me a whore for enjoying the attention I got when I dressed up, for dancing and laughing with others. He'd made me believe that I didn't deserve to be happy, that I wasn't good enough. And worse than all that, I had believed him.

But now, spinning around in Diago's arms, I felt like I was reclaiming that part of myself, the part that had been buried under years of manipulation and pain. I danced until I couldn't breathe, until my sides ached and my cheeks hurt from smiling. And through it all, Diago was there, watching me with an intensity that made me feel like the most exquisite woman here.

As the music slowed, I noticed a group of people gathered near an archery range, shooting arrows at targets set up at various distances. My competitive spirit stirred, and I turned to Diago with a grin. "Do you see that?" I pointed to the archery range. "If you win, you get to fuck me any way you'd like."

Diago raised an eyebrow, his smile turning wicked. "Any way?"

"Anything goes," I said, feeling a thrill at the challenge. "But if I win, I get to do whatever I want to you."

He laughed, the sound rich and full of promise. "Sounds like a win-win to me."

We made our way over to the archery area, where an attendant sized us both for bows. I went first, taking an arrow and nocking it with practiced ease. I hadn't shot an arrow in years, but the feel of the bow in my hand, the tension in the string, it all came back to me like muscle memory.

I released the first arrow, and it hit the middle ring, not quite the bullseye, but close. I jumped up and down in excitement, feeling a rush of adrenaline. My second shot was even closer, just a hair's breadth from the center.

"You're a natural," Diago said, his voice full of admiration.

I took a deep breath and aimed my third arrow, focusing all my energy on hitting the mark. When I released, the arrow flew straight and true, landing dead center in the bullseye. I twirled with excitement, unable to contain the joy bubbling up inside me. I hadn't felt this alive in years.

I took a mock bow and handed the bow to Diago. "Your turn," I said, giving him a playful smile. "Hope you like to swing, baby."

A spark of heat flared between my legs at the thought of what that could mean. I had never had sex on a swing before, but now I was hoping Diago was better at archery than me.

Diago stepped up to the line, his movements confident and controlled. He drew the bowstring back and released the first arrow. It hit the bullseye dead center. He shot the second with the same precision, and then, with a cheeky grin, he turned slightly, not even looking at the target as he loosed the third arrow. It, too, hit dead center.

"Impressive," I said, feeling the heat between us intensify. "I hope I know how to swing."

Diago leaned in close, his breath hot against my ear. "Oh, diosa, I'm going to fuck you so good, you'll never forget it."

A shiver ran down my spine as he took my hand and led me away from the fairgrounds, into a secluded grove of trees. There, hanging from a sturdy branch, was a sex swing, its leather straps and metal chains glistening in the dappled sunlight.

My heart raced with anticipation as Diago turned to me, his eyes dark with desire. "I'll help you out," he said softly, his hands already moving to lift my dress.

I let out a soft gasp as he slid the fabric up, revealing that I wasn't wearing any panties. My skin tingled under his touch, every nerve ending alive with anticipation. He helped me into the swing, his strong hands guiding me into place, securing the straps around my thighs, my calves, my feet, until I was suspended in the air, my most intimate parts exposed and vulnerable to him.

Diago's hands slid over my skin, his fingers tracing the curves of my hips, my thighs, before finding the wet heat between my legs. He dipped his head, and I felt his breath against my most sensitive spot. Then his tongue was there, licking, tasting me, his lips and tongue working in perfect rhythm to drive me wild.

"You taste so sweet," he murmured between licks, his voice a dark promise. "Like grapes and honey."

I moaned, the sound ripped from deep within me as pleasure exploded through my body. Every sensation was heightened, every touch sending electric pulses through me. I couldn't imagine coming this hard, but I did. My first orgasm hit me like a tidal wave, leaving me breathless and trembling in the swing.

Diago looked up at me, a satisfied grin on his face. "I hope you're not tuckered out yet," he said, his hands spreading my thighs wider, holding me as if I weighed nothing.

Before I could catch my breath, he slid into me, his cock filling me completely, the feel of him driving me wild all over again. I clawed at him, at the tree, desperate for more as the pressure and pleasure built within me, spiraling higher and higher until another thrust sent me over the edge again. This time, the orgasm was even more intense, a crescendo of pleasure that left me gasping for air.

Diago continued to thrust into me, deeper, his hands digging into my ass, pulling me closer to him as if he couldn't get enough. I was on the edge again, so close to that sweet release. "More," I panted, my voice desperate. "I need more."

He growled in response, thrusting harder, faster. He pulled out briefly, wetting his fingers in my slick heat before plunging back in. "I'm going to fuck your ass too, baby," he said, his voice rough with desire.

I nodded enthusiastically, the thought of it only adding to the fire inside me. "More," I begged. "I need more."

He found my tight, untouched hole and began rubbing circles around it, wetting the area with my juices before slowly pressing a finger inside. The sensation was overwhelming, his cock and finger moving in tandem, driving me to the brink of insanity with pleasure. The world around me exploded into a haze of pure bliss, my senses overwhelmed by the waves of ecstasy crashing over me.

Tears of joy, of pleasure, filled my eyes as I cried out, begging him not to stop. Diago continued to thrust into me, his cock filling me completely, stretching me to the point of sweet ecstasy. Every thrust, every movement sent me spiraling higher, lost in the pleasure that consumed me entirely. His fingers worked in perfect rhythm, teasing and stretching me in ways that made my body sing with pleasure. I had never felt anything like this before— so raw, so powerful, so completely overwhelming.

"You're so damn tight," Diago growled, his voice thick with desire as he continued to thrust into me. "All I want is to make you come again and again, until you can't take it anymore."

I was already on the edge, my body trembling with the need for release. His words pushed me even closer, the combination of his cock, his fingers, and the way he spoke to me sending me into overdrive. My body tightened around him, every nerve ending on fire as I approached another peak.

Diago's other hand found my clit, rubbing slow, deliberate circles that made me cry out in pure pleasure. The sensation was too much, too intense, and yet I craved more. I needed more.

"I can't—" I gasped, the words barely escaping my lips as I teetered on the brink of another orgasm. "I'm going to—"

"Come for me, Melanie," Diago whispered, his voice a dark, sensual command. "Let go. Give it to me."

His words were the final push I needed. With one last, deep thrust, my body exploded into the most intense orgasm I had ever experienced. I cried out his name, my entire being consumed by the pleasure that crashed over me in waves, drowning me in its intensity. I was completely lost in the sensation, nothing else existing except for this moment, this man, and the way he made me feel.

Diago continued to move within me, slowing his pace as I rode out the last tremors of my orgasm. He didn't stop, didn't pull away, his hands still holding me firmly as I came down from the high.

But just as I started to catch my breath, he began to move again, this time slower, deeper, driving me wild all over again. My body was already so sensitive, so overwhelmed, and yet every part of me craved more.

"I didn't say you could stop," I whispered, my voice shaky but filled with desire.

He smiled, a wicked grin that sent a shiver down

my spine. "I wouldn't dream of it," he replied, his voice thick with promise.

He started moving again, each thrust slow and deliberate. The slow pace was maddening, every inch of my body screaming for more, for faster, for harder. But he kept it slow, drawing out the pleasure, making me feel every single movement, every inch of his cock as it filled me.

His hand returned to my clit, rubbing those slow, agonizing circles that made my entire body tremble with need. I couldn't take it, the pleasure too intense, too overwhelming. My nerves were on fire, every touch, every movement sending electric pulses through me.

"I'm going to fuck you so good, Melanie," Diago whispered, his voice low and husky as he leaned in to kiss me deeply.

His lips found mine, his kiss slow and sensual, his tongue teasing mine as he continued to thrust into me. I moaned into his mouth, my hands gripping his shoulders, my nails digging into his skin as I rode the wave of pleasure.

He pulled back just enough to look at me, his eyes dark with desire. "You're mine, Melanie," he whispered, his voice filled with possessive heat. "Every inch of you belongs to me."

I nodded, unable to speak, my body already teetering on the edge of another orgasm. He reached up and pulled my dress down, exposing my breasts to the cool air. My nipples were hard, aching for his touch, and when he took one into his mouth, the sensation sent me over the edge again.

He sucked on my nipple, his tongue teasing the sensitive skin as he continued to thrust into me, harder, faster, his pace finally matching the desperate need that had built inside me. I was completely lost, every part of me consumed by the pleasure that he was giving me, that he was pulling from me.

My body tightened around him, every nerve ending on fire as I approached another peak. He moved faster, his cock driving into me with a force that made my entire body tremble. I was so close, so close to that final release that would send me spiraling into bliss.

With one last, deep thrust, I came again, my orgasm crashing over me like a tidal wave. Diago followed me, his own release finding him as he thrust deep into me one final time, filling me with his hot, pulsing cum. The sensation was incredible, the warmth of his release mixing with the pleasure of my own, leaving me breathless and trembling in his arms.

He held me there, in the swing, his body pressed against mine as we both caught our breath. The world around us seemed to slow, the sounds of the fair fading into the background as we stayed locked in each other's embrace.

When I finally found the strength to speak, my voice was barely more than a whisper. "That was... incredible."

Diago smiled, a soft, satisfied smile that made my heart flutter. "You're incredible, Melanie," he replied, his voice filled with genuine affection.

With a gentle touch, he helped me out of the swing, my legs still shaky from the intensity of our encounter. He scooped me up into his arms, carrying me through the trees to a nearby bed that hadn't been there before—a four-poster bed draped in soft, white linens, the mattress feeling like clouds beneath me as he laid me down.

He joined me on the bed, pulling me into his arms, holding me close as I drifted into a blissful, satisfied haze. The last thing I remembered before sleep claimed me was the feel of his warm body against mine, the sound of his steady breathing, and the knowledge that, for the first time in a long time, I had taken something for myself—something real, something beautiful.

And I wasn't about to let it go.

CHAPTER FOUR

*W*hen I woke next, I felt more rested than I had in years. For a moment, I just lay there, reveling in the warmth and comfort surrounding me. But as consciousness crept back in, I realized I wasn't alone. A strong arm was draped over my waist, the heat of another body pressed against my back. Panic flared—my first thought was of my ex—but then I remembered where I was, and who I was with. The tension melted away as I recognized Diego's familiar presence.

I turned carefully to face him, taking in the sight of his sleeping form. He looked peaceful, his chiseled features softened by sleep. His dark hair was tousled, and there was a hint of a smile on his lips, as if even his dreams were pleasant. My heart swelled with a mix of emotions—relief, contentment, and something deeper that I wasn't ready to name.

As if sensing my gaze, Diego stirred, his eyes fluttering open. When he saw me, that soft smile spread, and he tightened his arm around me, pulling me closer. "Good morning, beautiful," he murmured, his voice husky from sleep. He leaned in and pressed a gentle kiss to my forehead, then to my lips, a touch so tender it made my heart ache in the best way.

"Good morning," I replied, my voice still groggy. I let myself relax into him, enjoying the warmth of his body against mine.

Diego's hand traced lazy circles on my back, his touch soothing. "How do you feel?"

"More rested than I've felt in years," I admitted. "I could get used to waking up like this."

He chuckled softly. "I wouldn't mind that either."

I looked up at him, my curiosity getting the better of me. "How old are you, Diego?"

He raised an eyebrow, his lips quirking into a playful smile. "Does it matter?"

"Not particularly," I said, a grin tugging at my own lips. "But I am curious."

He paused for a moment, as if debating whether to tell me. Then, with a slight nod, he said, "I'm one hundred and forty-five."

I blinked, taken aback. I had expected something

unusual, but not quite that. "And you don't look a day over thirty-five," I teased.

He laughed, the sound rich and full. "Thank you. Now it's your turn. How old are you?"

I smiled, feeling a little more playful. "Old enough to have a daughter and an ex I was with for ten years."

Diego's expression turned serious, though the heat in his gaze never dimmed. "I'd do just about anything to spend ten years with you, Melanie."

His words sent a warm flush through me, and I looked away, feeling suddenly shy. "How does someone get work in a place like this?" I asked, trying to keep the conversation light. "Or are you just a figment of my imagination? My perfect man?"

Diego laughed, a deep, genuine sound that made me smile. His hand moved to stroke the curves of my belly, sending little shivers of pleasure through me. "I'm not a figment of your imagination, though everything else here is. The magic used to create this space is older than time. In fact, you have to have some magic in you in order for it to work at all."

I looked at him, intrigued. "So, do I have magic?"

He nodded, his eyes tracing the lines of my face as if he were committing them to memory. "Yes, Melanie. It courses along your skin, a subtle but powerful energy. It's part of what makes you so special."

I couldn't help but smile at that, enjoying the thought of having magic, of being more than just an ordinary woman. "Why are you here? Is this like a job? Do you come to the Arcane Room to... you know, fuck random people?" I asked the last part with a teasing lilt in my voice.

Diego smirked, shaking his head. "It's not quite like that. While some of the people you might encounter in the Arcane Room are from your memories, desires, or mind, others are real. We're connected in the same way you are. You created this space because it's what you needed, and I happened to be someone who could add to your life and pleasure. I came here because of the promise of someone who could add to mine too."

I considered his words, turning them over in my mind. "So, it's like a dating service? Or something like that?"

"Sort of," he said with a chuckle. "Things in the Shadow and Fae Realms are different than in the human world. The rules are made by beings who've never had to follow human laws. It's... more fluid, more about what you need at the moment than what society says you should do."

"The Fae Realm," I repeated, my curiosity piqued. "What's it like?"

Diego's eyes lit up as he began to explain, his voice taking on a tone of wonder. "The Fae Realm is a place of stories and belief. Everything there exists because someone, somewhere, believes in it. Magic, love, the universe itself—all of it is based on the power of belief. But sometimes, there are stories that hold just as much belief and love and hope in the hearts of people, but they don't fit into their reality. That's the Fae world. It's like ten hundred thousand stories woven together, expansive and vivid. The world is pure belief and magic, and it's intoxicating."

I listened, enraptured by his description. It sounded like a place out of a dream, a world where anything was possible. "Can people go there?" I asked, my voice soft with awe.

"Yes," Diego said, his voice taking on a more serious tone. "But people don't often come back. Before you go, you're asked to be sure—absolutely sure—that it's what you want, because once you cross that threshold, you may never return."

His words hung in the air, the weight of them sinking into me. I could sense the truth in what he was saying, as if the very air around us vibrated with the power of his belief. "And the Shadow World?" I asked, curious about the place where creatures of the night found sanctuary.

Diego's expression darkened slightly, though there was still a warmth in his eyes. "The Shadow World is where beings of the night are safe to be themselves. In the human world, they often have to confine themselves to human forms, and that can be taxing for creatures like griffons, dragons, deities, even shifters and vampires. They have to play by human rules, which isn't natural for them. In the Shadows, they're free to be who they truly are."

His words reminded me of something I had experienced years ago, something that had always seemed like a dream, but maybe wasn't. "When I was younger," I began, "I was driving home from work one night, up this huge hill. On one side of the road was a large wall of rocks, and on the other side was a drop-off, about a hundred feet down to a farm. I'd driven that road a thousand times before, but this night... something huge jumped down from the rocks into the middle of the road. I almost hit it. It was the biggest, hairiest, wildest thing I'd ever seen. It looked at me—almost man-like—then shifted to all fours and jumped down the hundred-foot drop. I just sat there, stunned, unable to figure out what it was or where it came from."

Diego listened intently, a knowing grin spreading across his face. "Sounds like you might have encountered a shifter... or maybe even a Bigfoot."

My eyes widened in surprise, excitement bubbling up inside me. "Is Bigfoot real?"

Diego laughed, a rich, warm sound that filled the room. "Does a vampire bite?"

I clapped my hands together, feeling almost giddy. "I always knew there was more to this world!"

"There's more than you'll ever fully understand," he said, his tone both teasing and sincere.

I paused, looking at him more seriously. "What about you? What are you?"

Diego smiled, a mysterious glint in his eyes. "Why don't you guess?"

I tilted my head, taking him in—his stillness, his strength, the way he moved with such quiet grace. I wasn't sure, but I knew he was something powerful. "Maybe... a mermaid? Or a wolf?"

He chuckled, shaking his head. "Neither. But I've always longed for the water, so I swoop at any opportunity to be in it." He leaned closer, his voice dropping to a whisper. "I'll give you a hint... I can fly."

I raised an eyebrow, feigning disbelief. "I can fly too, you know."

"With wings," he added, his smile widening.

I thought about the possibilities, my mind running through the creatures I knew. "A fairy?"

He shook his head, a gentle smile playing on his lips. "No, Melanie. I'm a gargoyle."

The realization settled over me, and I felt a thrill of excitement. I had always been fascinated by mythical creatures, and gargoyles were some of the most intriguing. "Gargoyles are protectors," I said softly. "Were you sent to protect me?"

Diego's expression softened, and he reached out to stroke my cheek. "It's what you desired most of all when you entered the Arcane Room. You wanted to feel safe, protected, loved. You wanted to let your guard down and just be yourself for a while, without feeling guilty."

Tears welled in my eyes, and I nodded, unable to speak. He was right—I had come here seeking all of those things, and more. "I thought gargoyles only protected against evil spirits," I said, my voice thick with emotion.

Diego shook his head, a tender smile on his lips. "That's a common misconception. We protect against evil… and against the assholes of the world too. We're guardians."

My heart swelled with gratitude and something deeper, something I couldn't quite name. I cuddled up closer to him, feeling the connection between us deepen. "So, you're my guardian gargoyle," I whispered, feeling a sense of peace I hadn't known in years.

Diego smiled, his arms wrapping around me, holding me close. "I'll be anything you need, baby."

And in that moment, I believed him. For the first time in a long time, I felt truly safe, truly cared for.

And I knew, deep down, that I wasn't alone anymore.

CHAPTER FIVE

*D*iego's voice was like velvet as he asked, "Is there anything else you want to do here, Melanie?"

I looked at him, his dark eyes filled with warmth and something more, something that made my heart flutter. The Arcane Room had already given me so much—a sense of safety, pleasure, and the feeling of being truly seen. But there was one thing I wanted more than anything else right now.

"If I can do anything," I said softly, "then I just want to spend a little more time with you."

His smile widened, a look of pure adoration in his gaze. "Of course, my love. Whatever you need."

I didn't hesitate. I moved quickly, pushing him back onto the bed and swinging my leg over him, straddling his hips. The warmth of his body against mine sent a thrill through me, and I could feel the heat between my legs growing as his erection pressed against me, thick and hard. The sensation of his desire, so tangible, made my own pulse quicken.

My hands slid over his chest, feeling the strength of his muscles beneath my fingers. I leaned down, kissing him deeply, pouring every ounce of my passion into that kiss. His hands found my hips, holding me close as he kissed me back with equal fervor. But this time, I wanted to take control—I wanted to show him just how much I desired him.

I broke the kiss, moving my lips down his neck, savoring the taste of his skin. His breath hitched as I kissed along his collarbone, then lower, my tongue tracing a path down his chest, over the ridges of his abs, until I reached the waistband of his pants.

Diego's cock strained against the fabric, the sight of it making my mouth water. I undid his pants with deliberate slowness, savoring the anticipation, then slipped them off, leaving him fully exposed. His erection stood proud, thick and pulsing with need, and I couldn't resist running my tongue along its length, tasting him, savoring the way he groaned at the contact.

"You're so hot and wet," he murmured, his voice thick with desire. "I can feel how much you want this."

I didn't respond with words. Instead, I positioned

myself over him, guiding his cock to my entrance. I lowered myself onto him slowly, taking my time to feel every inch as he filled me, stretching me in the most delicious way. The sensation was intense, almost overwhelming, and I couldn't hold back the moan that escaped my lips as he sank into me completely.

Diego's hands slid up to cup my breasts, massaging them gently as I began to move. I rode him slowly at first, savoring the way he felt inside me, every thrust sending ripples of pleasure through my body. My breasts bounced in time with my movements, and he groaned in appreciation, his hands squeezing them gently.

"You're extraordinary, Melanie," he murmured, his voice filled with awe. "So beautiful, so perfect."

His words fueled my desire, giving me the confidence to ride him harder, faster. The build-up inside me was undeniable, a tight coil of pleasure that grew with every thrust. Diego's hand slid down between us, finding my clit and rubbing slow, teasing circles around the sensitive bundle of nerves. The pleasure was almost too much, my body trembling as he coaxed me closer to the edge.

"Come for me, baby," he whispered, his voice thick with need. "I want to watch you scream my name. Your pleasure is my pleasure, Melanie. Nothing turns me on more than you."

His words, combined with the way he touched me, pushed me to the brink. I rode him faster, harder, the friction sending shockwaves of pleasure through me. "You're the sexiest creature I've seen in my one-hundred and forty-five years," he continued, his voice a low growl. "Only you, Melanie."

I couldn't hold back any longer. The pressure inside me built to a fever pitch, and I knew I was close, so close. "Will you... will you fuck me while flying?" I asked, breathless with anticipation. "In your arms?"

He looked at me, his eyes darkening with desire. "It's dangerous," he said, his voice husky. "But for you, anything."

Before I could respond, Diego's strong arms wrapped around me, holding me close as his wings unfurled behind him. They were massive, seven feet on either side, thick and powerful. The sight of them took my breath away, and I could feel my heart racing with both fear and excitement.

He flapped his wings, and we began to rise, hovering above the bed. The sensation of being lifted, of flying while still connected to him, was incredible. His cock remained deep inside me, the thrusts synchronized with each powerful flap of his wings.

We hovered higher, the air around us cool and exhilarating. The feeling of him inside me, combined with the thrill of being airborne, was almost too much to bear. Every flap of his wings drove him deeper into me, every thrust sending me closer to the edge.

"I'm going to come," I gasped, the intensity of it all making me tremble in his arms.

"Yes, baby," he growled, his voice filled with raw need. "I need you to do that. I want you to feel everything, Melanie. Scream for me."

His words pushed me over the edge. My orgasm hit me like a tidal wave, the pleasure so intense that I couldn't hold back the scream that tore from my throat. My body tightened around him, every muscle quivering as I came hard, my climax sending shockwaves through me.

Diego's thrusts grew more frantic, more desperate, as he followed me into ecstasy. With one final, powerful thrust, he came inside me, filling me with his warmth. The sensation was pure magic, the heat of his release blending with the euphoria of my own.

He flapped his wings slowly, lowering us back to the bed. When we touched down, he laid me gently on the soft mattress, his arms still wrapped around me. I was breathless, my body trembling with the aftershocks of the most intense orgasm.

Diego looked down at me, his eyes filled with a tenderness that made my heart ache. "You're incredible," he whispered, pressing a soft kiss to my forehead. "I hope that was everything you wanted."

I could only nod, still too overwhelmed to speak. The whole experience had been absolute magic, something out of a dream that I never wanted to end.

He held me close, his wings folding back as he cradled me in his arms. And as I lay there, safe and warm in his embrace, I knew that this was more than just a fantasy. It was a connection, something real and profound that had awakened something inside me I hadn't known was still there.

CHAPTER SIX

*a*s I lay in Diego's arms, my fingers traced the edges of his magnificent wings. The feathers were glorious—silver, shimmering, each one catching the light as though they were made of pure starlight. I marveled at their beauty, feeling a deep connection to this incredible being who had shown me more in these few hours than I had experienced in years.

One of the feathers loosened and drifted down, catching in the slight breeze before settling gently on the ground. Diego reached down, plucking the feather from the earth, and then held it out to me.

"This is for you," he said softly, his voice tinged with the bittersweetness of the moment. "To remember me by."

I took the feather, my heart aching as I wrapped

my fingers around the delicate silver quill. The reality that our time together was coming to an end settled over me like a heavy blanket. It felt like we had been together for days, but somewhere in the back of my mind, I knew Ms. Vesper had said it would only be twenty minutes. Twenty minutes that had changed everything.

"It's the best twenty minutes of my life," I whispered, the words catching in my throat.

Diego smiled, his eyes soft as he looked at me. "I want you to remember how strong you are, Melanie. You are an incredible woman, capable of anything you put your mind to. No person has control over you. You fight for Rose, and everything you endure is for her betterment. She's worth it, but so are you. You deserve better than the life you've been given. You didn't deserve his hate, his anger, his manipulation. You deserve love, Melanie. You deserve all the happiness in the world, and every pleasure that comes with it."

His words wrapped around me, filling the cracks in my heart with warmth and reassurance. I had needed to hear those things for so long, but it wasn't until Diego said them that I truly believed them.

"Will I ever see you again?" I asked, my voice small, my heart aching at the thought of saying goodbye.

Diego's eyes darkened with emotion as he gently

cupped my face in his hands. "I hope so, Melanie. In another time, another place, I hope our paths cross again. And when they do, I'll wrap my arms and wings around you, and you'll forever know that you are safe."

He leaned in, pressing a final, lingering kiss to my lips, filled with a promise that transcended words. "Until that time, just know that I'm watching over you."

The world around us began to shimmer, the edges blurring as the magic of the Arcane Room slowly unraveled. I blinked, and suddenly, I was no longer in Diego's arms. Instead, I was lying in the leather chair in the white room of the Arcane Room. The air was still, the only sound the soft hum of the world outside.

I sat up, disoriented for a moment, my heart pounding as I tried to hold onto the feeling of Diego's warmth, the memory of his touch. But then I noticed something that made me freeze—a single silver feather resting in my lap. Chills ran up and down my spine as I realized that perhaps it wasn't a dream after all. Perhaps all of it, including Diego, had been real.

Ms. Vesper stood in the doorway, watching me with a knowing smile. "How are you feeling, Melanie?"

I picked up the feather, twirling it between my

fingers, feeling the weight of its reality. "Thank you," I said, my voice filled with emotion. "That was the kindest gift anyone's ever given me. You've helped me find the strength to keep pushing forward."

Ms. Vesper's smile widened, a look of pride in her eyes. "I'm glad to hear that, my dear. You've always had that strength inside you. Sometimes we just need a little reminder."

"Thank you," I whispered, gratitude swelling in my chest.

As I left the Arcane Room, the sun felt warmer on my skin, the air fresher in my lungs. For the first time in years, I felt like myself—confident, loved, and whole. The weight of the past ten years didn't seem so heavy anymore, and I knew that whatever came next, I was ready to face it.

I looked at the clock in my car as I got in. Only an hour and a half until I got to pick up Rose. A smile spread across my face as I thought about her, my precious daughter, and the future that awaited us both. And as I drove away, the silver feather tucked safely in my bag, I knew that no matter what, I wasn't alone.

If you enjoyed the Queen of Pentacles, be on the look out for Melanie's next appearance. Sign up for my newsletter to be the first to know about all my new releases. I'm also giving away a free unpublished ebook when sign up!

Jax Wilder

Check out Knead You Now, from my Coral Cove series.

Accepting his help came with an unexpected proposition— pretending to be his girlfriend...

DOROTHEA

Early mornings, delicious pastries, and the comforting rhythm of kneading dough make up my world. But everything I've worked for is threatened I'm desperate and out of options. I turned to the town's most feared and successful lawyer, for help. Little did I know that accepting his assistance would come with an unexpected proposition – pretending to be his girlfriend.

Lorenzo

Coral Cove was supposed to be a fresh start, a place where I could build my own practice and escape the shadow of my overbearing father. But when he decides to visit, I need to show him I've settled down. Our arrangement is simple – I'll help her keep her bakery, and she'll help me convince my father that I'm living the life he envisions. But as we spend more time together, our fake relationship starts to feel all too real.

Join Dorothea and Lorenzo on a journey of love, trust, and the power of community. Will they be able to keep up their charade without falling for each other, or will the lines between reality and pretend blur beyond recognition?

Perfect for fans of heartfelt romances, small-town settings, and delicious baked goods. If you love stories where love blossoms in the most unexpected places, "Knead You Now" will warm your heart and satisfy your craving for a sweet romance.

ALSO BY JAX WILDER

CORAL COVE SERIES

Sleighed by Love

Harvesting Love

Dawning Desire

Knead You Now

Love Rewound

TAROT FANTASIES SERIES

The Devil's Temptations

Strength of The Beast

Hanged Passions

Six of Cups

Death's Embrace

Additional Books by
Rainbow Quartz Publishing

MIRANDA LEVI

From A Youth A Fountain Did Flow

The Sea Withdrew

A Tear In Time

Mo(ther) Na(ture)

In Orion's Hands

JACKSON ANHALT

From The 911 Files

LORELAI HAMILTON

Teenage Tarot

Tarot Tales and Magic Spells

Find Your Bliss

Teenage Witch's Grimoire

Tarot Reflection Journal

Tarot Refection Journal Coloring The Tarot

The Eclectic Witch's Grimoire

Dream Journal

Arcane In Verse

ISLA WATTS: A FAIRY BAD DAY

Surprise! You're a Vampire

Gorgeous, Gorgeous, Gorgons

Mork The Handsome Orc

Adopted By Werewolves

Bite Me If You Can

That's The Spirit!

ROSE DAWSON'S BOOK JOURNALS: MY TIME WITH THE FAIRIES

Enchanted Escapades

Enchanted Escapades

Dewey Decimal Diaries

Siren's Songbook

Pride and Prejudice

Bibliophile's Bounty

Book of Books Journal

Pages & Passages Reading Journal

Bookworm's Companion Reading Journal & Tracker

ABOUT THE AUTHOR

Jax Wilder is a passionate romance author hailing from a charming small town nestled in the picturesque Pacific Northwest. With a heart full of love and an unyielding belief in the power of happily ever afters, Jax weaves enchanting tales of love and connection that leave readers captivated.

Jax's novels are a reflection of her commitment to celebrating the magic of love, and her characters' journeys mirror the warmth and happiness she has found in her own life. Join her on the enchanting journey of love, passion, and enduring connection through her heartfelt romance novels.

Jax Wilder